JUNGLE TREK

Story by Dianne Wolfer
Illustrations by Mark Wilson

PM Extras Chapter Books
Sapphire

U.S. Edition © 2006 Harcourt Achieve Inc.
10801 N. MoPac Expressway
Building #3
Austin, TX 78759
www.harcourtachieve.com

Text © 2003 Cengage Learning Australia Pty Limited
Illustrations © 2003 Cengage Learning Australia Pty Limited
Originally published in Australia by Cengage Learning Australia

2 3 4 5 6 7 8   1957   14 13 12 11 10
4500206462

Text: Diana Wolfer
Printed in China by 1010 Printing International Ltd

Jungle Trek
ISBN 978 0 75 789254 7

Contents

CHAPTER 1

No Buts!

"But what will we do each day?"

"I told you, David, we'll be hiking. I'll be taking photos for the magazine. It won't be easy. Some days we'll be walking from dawn till dusk."

"Do I *have* to go?"

"We've already been through this . . ."

"Why can't I stay with Grandma?"

"Ten days is too long," Mom replied. "You know she hasn't been well."

"What about Jared's family. They like having me."

"Not for ten days!"

"But . . ."

"No buts, David. It's already organized."

Once Mom gets *that tone* in her voice, there's no point arguing. I slammed the kitchen door and went outside to shoot a few baskets. I knew there was nothing I could do to make her change her mind.

The next day I heard Mom on the telephone confirming our tickets with the travel agent.

"We'll be joining the group in Port Moresby. Yes, two tickets. One for my son and one for me. No, he's twelve. Yes, he's very fit. I'm sure he'll be able to cope . . ."

"Where's Port Moresby?" I asked Mom after she'd hung up.

"Port Moresby is the capital of Papua New Guinea. We'll stay there overnight before catching a smaller plane into the mountains."

Mom is a wildlife photographer. She specializes in insects, and Papua New Guinea has the best bugs in the world! A nature magazine has commissioned an article on the insects that live along some famous walking trail. Mom will be snapping pictures of butterflies, but there's an endangered beetle she's also hoping to find.

Mom's been planning this trip for months. I was sure that somehow I'd be able to get out of going. Unfortunately that's not looking likely.

"Mom, I spoke to Jared," I said casually. "His family isn't doing anything during those weeks. He reckons his dad will need help with hay baling . . . "

"David, the answer is no! I want us to go together. A mother-and-son adventure. It'll be fun."

Hiking through muddy, mosquito-infested jungle—I don't think so! I stormed outside again with my basketball.

Bang, bounce, bang. Maybe I can break my hoop record. *Bang.* It isn't fair! Just because Mom wants to go and take photos, I have to get dragged along.

Bang, bounce. If Dad was alive, I bet he'd let me stay home! *Bang, bounce, bang . . .*

CHAPTER 2

Bug Fanatics

Okay, I have to admit, the flight was pretty cool.

They showed a movie and the meals came on little trays with lots of small packets and containers. The flight attendants kept offering me lemonade and juice, but the best thing was flushing the toilet. It sounded supersonic!

By the time we landed in Port Moresby I was *almost* happy that Mom had made me come along. Almost, but not quite.

The tour organizer met us in the arrival hall. What a place!

There were people everywhere balancing bags of groceries. They had the most interesting hair styles, too! Masses of thick, black curls decorated with bright beads, and hats made from cuscus fur. I flicked my limp bangs off my face and felt totally jealous.

A mini-bus whisked us through the dusty streets to our hotel, and somehow managed to avoid the dogs and people stepping out in front of us.

The hotel had a pool, so that's where I spent the afternoon. At 5:00 p.m. Mom said I had to go with her to the hike briefing.

There were six others in the group. All bug fanatics! Did I mention that this trek was specially designed for insect enthusiasts? Mom reckons Papua New Guinea has more kinds of insects than any other place in the world. So not only will we be scrambling through the jungle for ten days, we'll be on a continual bug-hunt. I'll have to listen to endless conversations about wings and antennae and proboscises and leg segments . . . Boring!

The other trekkers were all Mom's age, but they seemed okay. After we introduced ourselves, the group leader began talking.

"We'll meet in the lobby at 5:00 a.m. The flight leaves at 6:00 a.m. and we'll need to check-in our food and daypacks," she said.

"Make sure you keep water, your camera, and any other essentials in your daypack. Once we reach Kokoda, we'll meet our porters, visit the museum, and then begin trekking. Any questions?" the group leader asked.

There were heaps. I sipped my drink and finished writing up the day's events in my journal.

Wednesday, 7:00 p.m.

Just as I suspected – there are no other kids in the group. Looks like I'm in for a boring ten days with bug-obsessed adults. One of the guys seems okay. At least he talked to me and listened. For all the interest the others showed, I might have been a common beetle!

At last they've stopped talking. My stomach's grumbling. It must be time for dinner . . .

CHAPTER 3

Too Easy?

The flight over the mountains was amazing. After waiting for hours at the airstrip, we piled into this little fifteen-seater airplane. I sat behind the pilot so I could watch everything he did. He really knew his stuff. As we came in to land, we were surrounded by clouds. He banked steeply. It felt like we were falling through the air. Mom looked worried, but after a few ear-popping minutes, we came out below the cloud cover in time to spiral down, line up with the runway, and land. It was the best flight ever!

We met out porters on the airstrip. Luke was my helper. He's only six years older than me. I felt mean having him carry my gear, but Luke just laughed and told me how much he loved being a porter.

"Not many jobs here," he said. "Good pay, fresh air, interesting people. Too easy . . ."

I watched him lift my backpack and stroll up the first steep hill. Easy, I thought, as sweat poured down my face. Easy, I wondered, as I puffed along behind . . .

Phew! Despite all the hours I had spent training, this was not easy for me at all.

"How are you doing?" Mom asked as we flopped onto a couple of logs for a break.

"Getting there," I gasped.

"Good for you," she whispered. "I'm very proud of you."

I never know what to say when Mom gets mushy, so I offered her some of my snack bar.

"No thanks, David. I'm going to see if I can find any butterflies. You enjoy it."

The head porter led the adults on a short insect search. As they lifted rotting logs and scratched at the bark of trees, I took out my journal.

Thursday – Day 1 of the Hike

It's not too bad so far. Luke is pretty good company. He was telling me about his village. He says we'll reach it in two days. He says there is a school there. The way he spoke it sounds like that's something unusual . . .

"David, quick!" It was Mom. I dropped my journal and raced toward her.

"Are you okay?"

"Yes, look! It's a Giant Spiny Stick Insect."

What? I looked. There they were, six adults *oohing* and *aahing* over this long skinny bug. Mom was focusing her camera and clicking madly. In between shots the group leader measured the bug's length. Hans, the tall man who had asked me my name, was almost swooning with delight. I looked at Luke and rolled my eyes. We tried not to laugh.

CHAPTER 4

Falling

Friday – Day 2 of the Hike

Luke's really funny. We tell each other jokes. He's smart, too, even though he only went to school until fourth grade. After that he had to help his dad in the village garden. Luke's been a porter for almost a year now and this is his eleventh trek. He has an amazing bush knife (everyone here has one). He used it to cut a walking stick for me. We'll be at Luke's village tomorrow. He has another bush knife at home. He said I can use it, if it's okay with Mom . . .

Saturday – Day 3 of the Hike

We're getting into a routine. Up early, hike til lunchtime, have a look around for beetles and butterflies, then hike until evening. My legs don't ache as much, and sometimes it's almost fun (not that I'll tell Mom that). I've been spending most of my time with Luke. We walk ahead. That way I can pretend I'm not with the bug maniacs.

"David, can you help me?"

Mom was struggling to wrap a plastic sheet over her daypack. She was worried about the humidity affecting her expensive lenses, and this soaking rain wasn't helping. I tied the edges so that it wouldn't fly off.

"Thanks, David. That's better."

The group leader called us together. "This rain has made the track more dangerous than usual," she said. "There are two steep downhill sections ahead. We'll be dropping 850 yards in altitude. Please watch every step. Try not to slip, and stay near a buddy."

I looked at Luke. He grinned. We hoisted our loads and began hiking.

"Did you hear the one about the teacher?" Luke asked. He chuckled. "This is my sister's favorite joke . . ."

I smiled and waited for him to continue.

"What did the teacher say when her eye rolled down the hill?"

"I don't know. What?"

"Oh no, there goes another pupil!"

I groaned. "That's terrible. Okay, now I've got one for you. What did the monster say—"

"Help!"

The sudden cry silenced me. It was Mom! I dropped my daypack and ran back along the path, slipping and sliding through the mud.

CHAPTER **5**

Stranded

Mom was lying on the ground, biting her lip and clutching her ankle.

"Mom, are you okay?" She tried to smile, but it turned into a grimace.

"What happened?"

"I fell . . ."

"Help me take off her boot," I called to the others.

"Wait," Hans said. "I've done some medical training. If your mother has broken her ankle, it may be better to leave the boot on."

Hans lifted Mom onto a ground sheet and propped her against a log. "Can you move your foot?" he asked.

Mom gasped in pain as she tried.

"How far is the next village?" she asked.

"Another five hours' walk," the group leader said. Mom's face turned even paler.

"But there is an airstrip there," the group leader added. "I'll send someone ahead with a message." She turned to Mom. "It will be too late to airlift you out today, but it should be possible in the morning. It will be a long night, but I do have some ice packs."

"Can you hobble?" I asked.

Mom nodded. "I'll try."

Hans and a porter supported Mom's weight and she hopped along as best she could.

Whenever the path was wide enough, I walked beside Mom, telling jokes and stories, trying to keep her mind off the pain. She pretended she was okay, but I could see how much every dip in the track jolted her ankle.

We walked the last two hours in darkness. There was no moon, and the steady rain had soaked through us. We reached Lukc's village just after 8:00 p.m. A bed was already set up for Mom. She collapsed into a deep sleep.

Even though I was exhausted, it took me ages to get to sleep. Somewhere nearby a dog was howling. The local roosters seemed to be having a contest to decide the midnight squawking champion.

It rained all night.

Hans had to cut the laces to remove Mom's boot. The good news was that her ankle wasn't broken. It was a really bad sprain though.

We learned via the crackling radio that there was no chance of a plane landing in the morning. If the mist cleared, they'd try to schedule one the next day.

"We'll have to go on," the tour guide said. "There are not enough supplies for us all to stay longer. We'd be a burden on the village."

"But you can't just leave us," I said.

"You'll be fine, David." She handed me a few more ice packs for Mom. "Luke will stay with you. His father can coordinate the evacuation flight. Don't worry. You're in good hands."

"But . . ."

"You'll be fine. We'll see you in Port Moresby."

I watched them walk into the mist and thought that I had never felt so alone.

Mom put her hand on my shoulder. "I need to sleep," she said. "Will you be okay?"

I nodded and took a deep breath.

I sat by Mom's bedside for hours. At some point I must have dozed off. When I woke up, Luke was sitting by the door.

"My grandmother says you need a break."

"I'm okay."

Luke waved to someone outside and an old lady stepped in. She had a basin of water.

"This is Oala, my grandmother." I nodded to her and smiled. "She wants to know if you have soap?" Luke asked.

"Of course."

"Soap is expensive in our country," Luke said as he noticed my puzzled expression. "Grandma wants you to leave so she can help your mother take a bath."

I blushed. "Okay," I said.

CHAPTER 6

Show and Tell

I followed Luke out of the tent and into the courtyard. The rain had stopped, but thick mist still covered the mountains.

"When do you think it will clear?" I asked.

Luke shrugged. "Maybe tomorrow, maybe not."

"Where is the airstrip?"

"I'll show you."

We walked to the end of the village and Luke pointed. I stared at the airstrip not believing what I saw. It was on the side of a hill!

"You mean planes actually land there?"

Luke grinned. "It looks worse than it is. The pilot lands, taxis uphill to the flatter end, then turns the plane so it can't roll backward."

"And when they take-off again?"

He laughed. "That's even more exciting. The pilot turns the plane and immediately gains speed. There is a bump at the end of the strip that the plane bounces off at the last minute."

I swallowed.

"Don't worry," Luke said. "There have only been two accidents in the past five years . . ."

I didn't want to know any more. "Let's see the rest of the village," I suggested.

"Okay, I'll show you our school."

We walked through the village square and were followed by a group of dogs and young children. At school a class was in session, but the teacher stopped and welcomed us. I looked around. There were three worn-out books on a shelf. The teacher was using a wet cloth to write words on the blackboard.

"Don't you use chalk?" I asked.

"We ran out last year," Luke said.

"What about pencils and paper?"

"There is no money."

I tried to hide my shock. Then I remembered my journal.

"I have some paper and pens."

The kids sat up in excitement.

I ripped up my journal and handed out my pens, pencils, and colored markers. We spent the afternoon writing messages and copying each other's drawings. The teacher seemed thrilled at the interruption to his lesson. He kept shaking my hand and thanking me.

After school the kids took me into the jungle and showed me how to cut vines to weave into baskets. They taught me songs as we worked. Then we played scarecrow tag. Suddenly I remembered Mom.

"I have to get back," I said. I began feeling guilty that I'd forgotten about her for so long.

"Wait," Luke said. "There is one more thing I want to show you."

He led me to a small creek in the jungle. Luke parted some vines, then scooped up a beetle. It was huge with a beautiful metallic-looking carapace.

"Is this the one your mother has been looking for?" he asked.

"Yes, I think so!" I cried with bug-fanatic excitement. "It is a rhinoceros beetle. It looks like that rare one!"

Luke put the beetle into my hands, and we ran back to the village.

CHAPTER 7

Photos for the Magazine

When we got back, Mom was sitting on a blanket in the village square with a group of women around her. They were laughing and taking turns to pose in front of her camera.

"Mom, guess what?" I cried.

Mom turned. "Hi David!"

"I have a surprise for you." I opened my hand. "I think it's that rhinoceros beetle—the one you've been looking for! Luke took me to a place in the jungle. There are lots of them just down the hill. We could easily carry you . . ."

Mom reached for the beetle, and I saw tears in the corners of her eyes.

"Thank you, David. It's a beautiful beetle. It's the best gift . . ."

"But it isn't *the one*, is it?" I said.

"It's *like* the one we've been searching for. It's the same bright color . . ."

"Is it rare?"

Mom wrinkled her nose, "Well . . ."

"So, it's common then?"

"I wouldn't call it common." She reached out her hand. "Can I take a photo of you and Luke holding it?"

I hesitated. Mom knew I hated having my photo taken.

"Please."

How could I say no? Luke stood beside me. Then the village women decided to crowd around, too.

"Great," Mom called. "Smile."

She took a few shots, then leaned back exhausted. I felt tired, too.

"I was really hoping it would be the rare beetle," I muttered quietly to Mom. "Then you could still have taken photos for the magazine."

"That's just it," Mom cried, sitting forward with a fresh burst of energy. "I didn't have a chance to tell you. There's a wedding ceremony this afternoon. The women have been practicing singing songs. I've taken some fantastic shots of them dancing. The magazine will love them!"

I looked at the women decorated in their feathers and beads and shells. They looked so exotic with the lush, misty mountains as a backdrop.

"Then the trip hasn't been wasted?"

"Not at all. The photos will be great. I just hope the weather doesn't clear until after the ceremony."

Mom's wish was granted. We stayed one more night. Mom's backpack was filled with rolls of film ready to be developed at home.

Luke and his family sat on the airstrip with us as we waited to go. We heard the rumble of an engine edging nearer. It was time to say goodbye.

I took a deep breath as we stepped into the tiny airplane. Luke waved and said he'd be waiting for my first letter. We'd decided to write to each other. I hadn't told him that I also planned to send a box of books, pens, and toys to the village school.

As I helped Mom into her seat, she squeezed my hand. "Are you glad you came?" Mom asked.

The airplane was rolling down the runway. We picked up speed, hit the bump at the end of the airstrip, and the plane bounced into the air.

"Yeehah!" I squealed.

Then I turned back to Mom and grinned. "Very glad!" I said. "It's been the best mother-and-son time ever!"